C00 791 668X

KU-750-625

For Emily.

S.D.

For Aisling, Isabel, Leo and Des and especially, David.

J.L.

Published in 2017 by Golden Key Publishing.

56 Holmpatrick, Skerries, Co. Dublin, Ireland. Tel. +353 1 849 0598, info@goldenkey.ie

www.goldenkey.ie   www.gringerthewhinger.com

Text © Jane Landy

Illustrations © Sheena Dempsey

Designer: Acrobat Design.   Printed in Ireland by Turners of Longford.

All rights reserved. No part of this book may be transmitted, printed, copied, reproduced or stored in an information retrieval system in any form or by any means, graphic, electronic, or mechanical, including photocopying, taping or recording, without the prior written permission of the publishers.

ISBN 978-0-9553298-9-0

GRINGER THE WHINGER

LEISURE AND CULTURE DUNDEE	
C 00791668X	
Bertrams	18/12/2017
	£16.00
CSIDE	

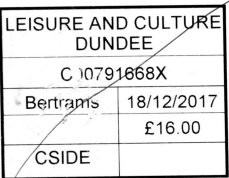

Jane Landy & Sheena Dempsey

Golden Key
Publishing

Gringer the Whinger lived down by the sea.
A whinging cantankerous dragon was he.

He loved to eat food and to pester our Mum.
Each day at mealtimes to our house he'd come.

And whenever we fought ...   ... and whenever we cried

Gringer the Whinger appeared at our side.

"Oh Mammy, oh Mammy, oh Mammy," said he,
"I want every bit of Isabel's tea."

"Oh Gringer," cried Mammy, "please go away."
"We really don't want you in our house today!"

"Weh weh," he would whinge

and "weh weh," he would say

But whatever she did, that dragon would stay.

"Eat up your fish now," said Mammy to us.
"Finish those peas and don't make a fuss."

But we didn't like peas and we didn't like fish
So we pushed them around and around in the dish.

"Now Mammy," said Gringer, "just listen to me.
I'm hungry and desperate for a lovely green pea."

"Go back to your own house!" cried Mammy all red.

"I will not," said Gringer, "until I've been fed."

Just then in came Daddy, so tired and so grim.

"Good heavens," he groaned, "don't tell me it's him!"

He picked up the brush and he opened the door
And swooshed Gringer out with a terrible roar!

But **we** really wanted Gringer to stay

And felt very cross that they'd sent him away.

Well, we ate up our food

and ran straight outside.

Had Gringer the Whinger found somewhere to hide?

The garden was empty but ever so high,
We could see Gringer - a speck in the sky.

We sighed, then we smiled, then we started to grin,
"When Gringer comes back then **we'll** let him in!"